Andrea Griffing

SO-EGQ-463

THE RIDDLE ZOO

illustrated by Giulio Maestro

E. P. DUTTON · NEW YORK

Library of Congress Cataloging in Publication Data

Zimmerman, Andrea Griffing.   The riddle zoo.

Summary: A collection of animal riddles such as "Why
are rats so unhappy? They're always down in the
dumps." and "What wakes up a farmer? An alarm cock."
1. Riddles, Juvenile.   2. Animals—Anecdotes, facetiae,
satire, etc.   3. Puns and punning.   [1. Riddles.
2. Animals—Anecdotes, facetiae, satire, etc.]
I. Maestro, Giulio.   II. Title.
PN6371.5.Z5   818'5402   81-3151
ISBN 0-525-38300-X   AACR2
ISBN 0-525-38299-2 (pbk.)

Published in the United States by Elsevier-Dutton
Publishing Co., Inc., 2 Park Avenue, New York, N.Y. 10016

Published simultaneously in Canada by Clarke,
Irwin & Company Limited, Toronto and Vancouver

Editor: Ann Troy   Designer: Giulio Maestro

Printed in the U.S.A.   First Edition
10 9 8 7 6 5 4 3 2 1

To David

What do monkeys do at feeding time?

They go bananas.

Why was the buffalo so careful when she chewed off a mouthful of grass?

She didn't want to bite the dust.

Why did the firefly flunk out of school?

He wasn't too bright.

What did the lobster say to the crab
who was eating all the food?

Hey, don't be so shellfish.

What animal never gets old?

A gnu.

What's tall, has spots, and wears
a sheet over his head?

A giraffe on Halloween.

What animals do baby monsters
play with?

Rattlesnakes.

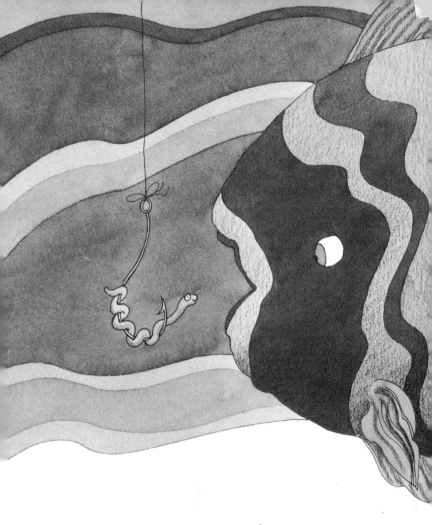

Why didn't the fish eat the worm
on the hook?

*She was afraid there might be
a catch.*

What does a porcupine cover
himself with at night?

A quilt.

On what horse would you get
all wet when riding?

A sea horse.

Why did the hippopotamus leave school carrying a chair?

The teacher told him to take a seat.

What did the dolphin say when she bumped into her friend?

I didn't do it on porpoise!

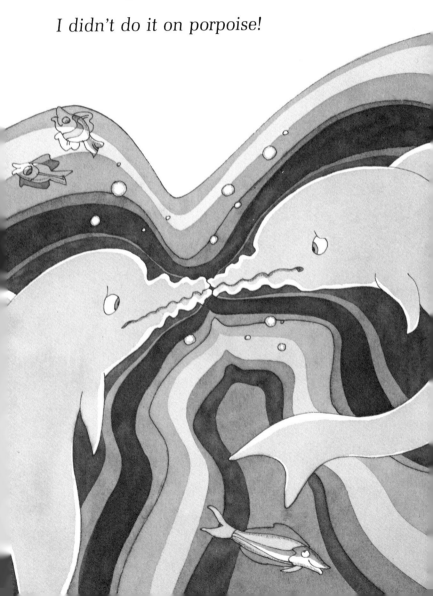

What animal is always nagging?

A badger.

How many paws does a lion have?

One (one paw and one maw).

How did the polar bear and the seal become friends?

They broke the ice.

What animal needs to wear a wig?

A bald eagle.

Why is a snake considered thrifty?

Because she can make both ends meet.

How do vampire bats feel when they get hungry?

Bloodthirsty.

Why was the tree sorry the woodpeckers came to dinner?

He got stuck with the bill.

Why didn't the pig go to the doctor when she had a cold?

She didn't want to be cured.

Why did the mule like to play soccer?

He got a kick out of it.

What's the best way to raise rabbits?

Put both hands around them and lift.

When are penguins afraid?

When they've got cold feet.

What do little snakes say when playing cops and robbers?

Fang, fang, you're dead.

Why didn't the tiger cub fight when his mother wanted to wash him?

He knew he'd be licked.

Why was the sheep afraid of being sheared?

He knew it would be a close shave.

What wakes up a farmer?

An alarm cock.

What animal can you always count on?

An adder.

Why did the rhino flunk his driving test?

He had taken a crash course.

Why did the teacher keep the snake after class?

He refused to raise his hand.

How did the cat feel after
he was chased?

Dog-tired.

What kind of bird bakes bread?

A dodo bird.

Why did the seal carry her dinner
on the end of her nose?

She wanted a well-balanced meal.

What does a kitten say when
he hurts himself?

Me-OW!

How do wasps stay dry?

They always wear their yellow jackets.

What are the strongest creatures living in the sea?

Mussels.

Why do lions and tigers gossip?

Because they're so catty.

When does the cow blow her horn?

When she's stuck in traffic.

What creature is a big grouch?

A crab.

How do sandpipers feel on a
sunny day at the beach?

Piping hot.

What bird is always eating?

A swallow.

What animal is always in pain?

An *OWWWWWL*.

Why did the inchworm stay in the house?

He didn't want to set foot in the yard.

What did the snake write at
the end of the letter?

Love and hisses.

Why do giraffes talk too much?

Because they're long-winded.

What do you call a horse who travels by car?

A riding horse.

How do you know that snakes
tell lies?

They speak with forked tongues.

What animal puts everyone to sleep?

A boar.

What animal isn't trustworthy?

A cheetah.

What's big and gray and has tusks and a trunk?

A walrus going on vacation.

Why are rats so unhappy?

They're always down in the dumps.

When is a lobster like Christmas?

When he's got Sandy Claws.

What animal won't wear clothes?

A bear.

What fish loves mice?

A catfish.

How did the bird feel when he landed
on the porcupine?

Excited, like he was on pins and needles.

When is an elephant like a cute
little bunny rabbit?

When *he's wearing his cute
little bunny rabbit suit.*

What animal is always talking?

A yak.

What horse is missing
three-fourths of itself?

A *quarter horse.*

Why aren't dogs very good at answering riddles?

They can only make ruff guesses.